APPLES IN THE SKY

To Judy—

Keep watching for your apples in the sky!

Christina McDade
1989

a

Dedication

To Steven

*I know we will always be
each other's "Darling".*

b

APPLES
in the
SKY

By C.M. McDade

Jordan Valley Heritage House

APPLES IN THE SKY

Copyright 1989, by Christina McDade

Jordan Valley Heritage House
43592 Hwy. 226
Stayton, Oregon 97383

Manufactured in U.S.A.

Library of Congress Catalog
Card number: 89-084590

ISBN: 0-939810-12-3 (Paperback)

First Edition

d

Chapter 1

The distant scream of sirens grew louder and more persistant. The sound crept up until it surrounded me.

My faint glimmer of consciousness grew until my thoughts twisted and tangled in my mind.

"Is a fire nearby?" I wondered. "Was someone hurt?"

I became more uncomfortable with each second as the noise urged me to clear my head.

Gushes of wind that followed the roars of passing cars came at frequent intervals. I felt the wind play with my hair and caress my cheeks. The warm sun sent a bright orange through my eyelids.

Suddenly, a voice cleared some of the dizziness and confusion. It shouted orders and urgent warnings.

I slowly opened my eyes to a brilliant scene of flashing red and blue lights. On my right, police cars were parked alongside a busy highway. The sirens had ceased their piercing wail.

I gazed above me at a cloudless azure sky. I lay, apparently on the ground, aware of an ambulance next to me, displaying red letters that spelled out its name.

A man in a white coat appeared. He made his way to my side, where he leaned over me and pulled up a long, brown strap. He buckled it to another one and tightened them over my legs.

Hurriedly, he then snatched a green blanket from the back of the ambulance. As he unfolded it, my eyes drifted back to the police cars where a small crowd of people stood. I could hear their low murmuring voices. When I looked carefully, I noticed they all stared directly at me!

It was then I realized I didn't know where I was, or why they were staring.

I observed more as my thoughts became more acute. Again I glanced at the little group. This time I recognized my parents. They were wrapped in each other's arms and appeared quite distraught. They were talking to a policeman.

My mother's face was crimson, steaked with trails

of tears. My dad had a painfully somber expression etched in his brow. I had seen them look this way only once before. At a funeral.

With every second, I became more awake and more scared, but I never knew what was happening.

The man in the white coat opened the ambulance doors after arranging the blanket over me. Another man joined him and they positioned themselves, one on my left and one on my right. The two men lifted me up. But on what? I knew I was lying down, but where?

Frightening thoughts tumbled through my head until a fiery jolt of pain struck my body.

When I was half way into the ambulance, I caught one last glimpse outside. Before the doors shut behind me, things became clearer. As the sterilized odor closed around me, I remembered what I had seen.

There had been a cream colored station wagon in the ditch. Even with front end face down and the side crushed in, I knew it was our family car. Beyond it, evergreens had swayed and bordered the afternoon sky.

I remembered then. My parents, little sister, and two younger brothers had set out from home to Grandma and Grandpa's house for Sunday dinner. Riding along, I had fallen asleep, as usual. Then, there must have been an accident.

My body was seized again by great shocks of pain. They began in my legs and bolted up to my chest. I cried out in agony! The pain was pure torture as it lingered on mercilessly. I gritted my teeth, praying it would leave!

Finally, I could bear it no longer. I gave in to it, and as soon as I did, I was swallowed up by blackness.

****

Beep. Beep. Beep. Beep.

I wished my alarm clock would turn itself off and let me sleep.

Waves of thought gently coaxed my mind to release my dreams and allow me to wake up.

Another day was waiting for me.

Gradually, I thought more clearly. "Why does my alarm clock sound so different?" I wondered. "Why do I feel so light headed?"

I tried to get up. Normally, I would have swung my legs over the edge of my bed, sat up, and opened my eyes. But something was wrong. I knew there was a problem. I couldn't feel anything!

My ears picked up other sounds; voices, anxious voices. For the moment at least, I was not ready to open my eyes.

I thought back to my last waking moment. The car in the ditch, the looks on my parents' faces, and the ambulance. In a flash of alarming reality, it all came back to me.

For a brief moment I relaxed in the comforting thought that it had all been a crazy dream. But if it had been a dream, why couldn't I move?

It was then I opened my eyes. When I saw the hospital room, I realized it had all been real. Panic raced through me!

Doctors and nurses rushed around doing things. There was an emergency, and I was it! Beeping and blinking machines surrounded me.

I wondered if they were aware that I could hear what they were saying. I thought not.

"The blood will be here any minute," somesome said.

"We have to have it now!"

"Couldn't either of her parents help?"

"No. She's a rare blood type."

"We have a problem here, doctor. Her blood pressure is dropping."

"We're losing her!"

I was dying? My thinking became blurred. The

numbness that had devoured my body was reaching my mind! I felt nothing except the warm tears falling from my eyes.

"The blood is here!"

"Is that all there is?" someone asked. "We'll need more!"

"This is all there is for now."

My eyes followed a nurse as she swiftly hung the container of blood in place. I looked to the side, seeing my own blood on the bed beneath me.

I watched as long as I could. Their white figures moved around the room. Then it all began to get dim.

Shadows of faces stood over me. The beeping machine seemed to be beeping slower. Now and then my vision cleared enough to see concerned eyes staring into mine. The room was filled with quiet and more shadows.

Even though my eyes were open, they must have thought I was unconscious.

A doctor stood looking down at me. I noticed his hands were clasped together in a tight fist.

Then it happened. No longer could I see, or hear.

I was nothing.

Chapter 2

As fast as I had lost consciousness, I regained it.
Or so it seemed. No longer was I under the desperate
faces of the doctors and nurses, but looking down on
them.

My mind became clear and I understood what had
happened. I knew I had just died, but I was not
afraid. I looked over the room, seeing the emergency
equipment and a man trying to pump life back into
my body.

Even if I could have, or known how to, I would
not have gone back. Death was not what I had expected.

I floated on the air, knowing I was there, yet not
being visible. I knew the lifeless body on the bed was
mine. It was a calm, airy feeling, so different from the

7

pain I'd left behind.

The people below worked frantically, trying to revive me.

"Come on Christina! Try!" one of them said.

A nurse reported, "It's been nearly two minutes now."

One doctor would not give up. "Please! Breathe!" He looked up at his assistant. "She's about the age of my own daughter." They continued working on my body.

Finally, the doctor stepped back and wiped his brow. I watched a nurse record the time of death as 4:25 p.m.

One by one they left the room with weary faces. They were so sad, thinking they had failed. I felt sorry for them. I wished I could tell them I was still there.

When I was alone, the room began to fill with a bright light. A shimmering silver glow surrounded me. For a moment, I was drowned in it.

Suddenly, I was standing in what looked like a long, dark cave. It stretched before me until it came to a round circle of sunshine at the end. The walls appeared to be rock, and were rough and jagged.

The air around me was pleasantly cool and sweet, touched with a faint fragrance of roses. I walked toward the sunlight, pulled by some unknown force.

A soft breeze danced around my face as I stepped along the mossy floor. As I neared the opening, I could see playful waves of light reaching inside. They flickered merrily on some tiny buttercups that grew there.

I caught a glimpse of what lay outside the tunnel. From where I stood, all I could see was the green of grass.

When I left the cavern, I found myself walking down a path. It was bordered by red roses and showed no signs of wear.

I sauntered easily along and drank in my surroundings. It reminded me of a giant park, flat and grassy, landscaped with a leafy tree here and there. Birds sang cheerful songs from their hidden branches. In the distance, a tiny pond rippled with the warm wisps of wind. A pair of swans glided along its wavy surface, bowing to the cattails with their long, graceful necks.

The garden seemed to stretch on forever under the sun and feathery white clouds. Eventually, it met the purple shadows of mountains that lined the horizon. Everything was so peaceful and perfect. It filled my heart with happiness.

I rambled on down the winding path. Abruptly, it

came to an end. Then I stood facing an apple tree. Looking up, I saw a few lacy blossoms, and curiously enough, shiny red apples on the same tree. I noticed a ring of bright yellow daffodils around the base of the trunk. Roots were poking up through the surrounding grass. All around me was beautiful, undisturbed nature, divinely tranquil.

Unexpectedly, a man walked out from behind the tree. As he came nearer I recognized him. Not from my life, but from photographs. He was my grandma's father.

Grandma had told me a thousand stories about her sweet old dad. She had said he had a mischievous twinkle in his eye when he spoke, and a grin that could set anyone at ease.

On his head was perched a narrow brimmed, white felt hat, tipped to one side. He was dressed in overalls and brown boots. His face, tanned from the sun, spread into a friendly smile as he greeted me.

"Well, hello there, Christina!" He called me by name as if he'd known me forever.

"Hello, Grandpa." I said. He did not seem surprised that I knew who he was.

"Looks like you're enjoying yourself!" He grinned.

"Yes, it's beautiful here. Is this heaven?" I asked.

He laughed heartily. For a moment I wasn't sure if I had really died!

"Yes, almost heaven." He answered. "This is as far as you'll be going this time."

"I don't understand," I said. "I did die, didn't I?" I began to wonder. I knew he had died many years ago. "I'm not going to stay dead?"

"That's right! Sometimes this happens. It's not your time to die yet. You are only fourteen, Christina!" He chuckled.

I didn't want to leave! I had never known such peace! This was paradise! How could I go back to all the pain and suffering that was waiting for me.

"I want to stay," I told him.

"Oh, don't worry. You'll be glad you returned." He reached for my hand and lightly placed it in his. I noticed his hands were soft, not callused as my grandma had described him. The scar on his cheek wasn't there either.

"You've got a lot of life yet to live. And there's work for you to do," he smiled.

"Please don't send me back!" I begged him.

"It's not up to me, Christina. It has to be this way. Life may be rough down there, but I'll be with you. Your family will be with you, too. You won't be alone. Don't worry! Keep the faith. Stevie needs you."

    I didn't have time to ask him why my little brother would need me. Before I could speak, he let go of my hand. As soon as he had, I was again enveloped with the same warm, bright light. I thought I heard him say, "Earn them apples now!" I wondered what he could have meant by that!

****

    I opened my eyes, now back in my body. Excruciating pain ripped through me. The seconds dragged on. I felt my temperature rising. Perspiration dripped from my forehead.

    I could see nothing except a white film over my face. I knew it was a sheet. Gathering up all my strength, I pulled it away.

    "I must have been dead for a long time," I thought.

    The room was dark except for a thin light that glowed through a small window in the door. Above it, I could barely make out a clock. It was 4:32; only seven minutes after I had watched the nurse record my time of death.

    Footsteps sounded in the hallway. I prayed they would stop, but they continued on and faded.

The pain grew worse! I had to stay awake so when they found me, they would know I was alive!

Suddenly, voices echoed in the hall. They grew louder. I tried to call out, but all that escaped my lips were quiet cries of anguish.

And then there was an answer to my prayer. The door flew open. In walked two men. They turned on the light. Instead of finding a dead, covered body, there I was, alive, ---my eyes pleading for help.

"She's alive!" one of them said. "Get the doctor!"

Then, once more I gave in to unconsciousness.

Chapter 3

(Monday morning)

"It's alright, Christina. Wake up. Everything's O.K." A nurse stood over me speaking softly, gently stroking my arm.

As I lay there, I wanted more than anything to go back to sleep, but the nurse kept pestering me.

"Wake up, Christina. You need to wake up now. You've had some surgery. You're all right." She continued shaking my arm. I hated it! I felt so groggy. I wished she would leave me alone. Finally, my eyes began to open, but just a little. I still felt sleepy.

"No," I thought, "I'm not ready to wake up. But the nurse insisted!

"Come on, honey. Keep those eyes open. Wake up." This time she shook me even harder.

Reluctantly, I opened my eyes. Although I felt strange, nothing hurt. I knew I was in a hospital. White, surrounded me. A white uniform, white sheets, white walls and on me, white bandages. My left leg was hanging in the air, like I'd seen on television. My right leg? It was there, wrapped up like a mummy. So was my left arm. There was an IV in my right arm.

As I looked at my situation, I didn't know whether to laugh or cry. When I tried to get some information out of the nurse, my words came out fuzzy. They rolled around peculiarly in my mouth. I got so frustrated and confused! I couldn't seem to spit the words out. But the nurse anticipated my questions.

She repeated what I thought she said earlier. "You've had some surgery, Christina. You're a lucky girl. You came in with lots of cuts and bruises, but you'll get well quickly. Don't be worried by all the bandages."

"What hospital is this?" I asked. This time my words made more sense, I think.

"Good, Christina, you're back with us," she said. "You are in Lost Lake General Hospital. This is the intensive care unit. You'll be here with us for a little while. When Dr. Honey comes in and gives his O.K., you'll be taken to your room."

"Dr. Honey?" I wondered if I'd heard right.

"Your parents are right outside. Do you feel like seeing them for a few minutes, Christina? They've been pretty worried. They want to see you."

"Are they alright? Was anyone else hurt?" I asked.

"I understand your little brother took a bump on the head. But besides getting a few bruises, everyone else is fine. You've got enough injuries for the whole family, Christina," she smiled.

I was not the only person in intensive care. Another nurse was tending a patient nearer the door.

"Gladys, would you please invite Christina's parents in? They're right outside."

Mom and Dad walked through the door a few seconds later. Although my mother tried to smile, it was no disguise for the pain in her tired eyes. Dad was different. He could find humor in every situation. This was no exception.

"Hey Christy, do you want to dance?" he smiled his broadest smile.

"Bert, I can't believe you!" my mother laughed.

"What happened to us?" I asked them. I had to know what was going on!

My mother glanced at the nurse as if to say, "What should we tell her?"

Just then the door opened and a tall, blonde man entered the room. He wore the classic stethoscope over a white jacket and was looking at a clipboard in his hand. He came toward us. Mom and Dad recognized him.

"How are you doing, Christina? Are you comfortable? Do you hurt anywhere?" he asked.

"My mouth is a little dry. Other than having my leg in the air, a needle in my arm, and not knowing what happened, I'm fine!" I answered. "Are you Dr. Honey?" I smiled.

"That's me! I'm a real sweet guy," he said as he shook one of my fingers. "Pleased to meet you, Christina."

"Are you the one who did this to me," I asked, looking at my airborne limb.

"No, Christy," Dad interrupted, "a drunk driver did this to you." This time he was serious.

I looked at my father. "What do you mean?"

"Christina, Dr. Honey told us you are going to your room on the sixth floor soon. We are going to go up with you, but then we're going to let you rest for a while. Dad and I are going over to Grandma and Grandpa's house to pick up Sara and Shawn. They are probably driving your grandparents crazy by now. We'll take them home and then we'll be back to tell you everything you want to know."

"This was weird," I thought. "Why wouldn't they tell me now?"

Dr. Honey left the room for a few minutes. He returned with two men in white jackets. They pushed me and my bed down the hall to the elevator. Mom and Dad walked along beside us. When we got to the sixth floor, they wheeled me in to room number 612. They shoved a bed aside making room for mine.

"Here we are," one of them announced. "Get some rest now," he said as he left the room, pushing the empty bed out.

Mom and Dad were anxious to leave. "We'll see you later, hon," Mom said.

"That is, if we can find your room when we come back," Dad teased. I could tell they were both tired. They gave me a kiss and walked out the door.

Once they'd gone, an uneasy loneliness set in. Everything had happened so fast! One minute I had been on my way to Grandma's house for Sunday dinner and the next, in a hospital bed. Had a drunk driver really caused the accident? And what about Steven? Mom and Dad hadn't mentioned him being at Grandma and Grandpa's house. The nurse had spoken of a bump on his head. I had a feeling it was more than that.

Suddenly, I remembered my great-grandfather. He had said that Steven would need me. But if Steven was hurt, what could I do? I knew I was in traction. And, I knew that it would take a long time to recover. How could I help him, when I couldn't even help myself!

A nurse hurried through the door. She smiled as as she passed my bed and disappeared behind a curtain. When I heard two voices I realized I had not been alone in the room.

I had been told to rest, but there were so many unanswered questions on my mind. Most of all, I couldn't stop thinking about Steven.

"Please God!" I silently prayed, "Let my little brother be all right!" But somehow, I knew he wasn't.

Chapter 4

"Christina." It was my mother's voice. "Dad and I are here, honey. Do you want to rest more before we talk?"

I had fallen asleep. When I remembered what they were going to tell me, my eyes popped open. Mom and Dad were standing by my bed. They both smiled, pulled up two nearby chairs, and settled down on them.

"Tell me what happened! What's wrong with Steven?" They looked at each other. "Did a drunk driver really hit us, Dad? What happened to me? How long will I be in the hospital?" There were tears in my eyes. I wasn't sure if I was ready for the answers to the questions I had asked!

Mom fixed her eyes on mine. "Christina, we feel

you should know everything. But, we don't want to upset you."

"Not telling me is more upsetting!" I replied.

"I know. The doctor told us not to tell you too much, ---but the doctor doesn't know you like we do. We know you can handle this," she explained.

"Please, Mom! I remember riding in the car, on our way to Grandma's house. I fell asleep. Then what happened?" I asked eagerly.

"All right. We were on our way to Grandma's house, almost to the turnoff, where that red barn is," she began slowly. I nodded, knowing the place she meant. "A blue pickup truck was coming toward us. Your dad noticed the guy was driving crazy, ---all over the road. Before Dad could get out of his way, the truck swerved across the line and hit us. It crashed into the back door, where you were sitting."

I recalled being in the back seat, leaning against the door. Steven had been asleep on my lap. My brother Shawn, sat next to us. Dad and Mom had been in front with my sister, Sara, between them.

For the first time, I noticed a square bandage on Dad's forehead. Mom had one of those stretchy bandages around her wrist, as if it had been sprained.

"There was nothing Dad could do, Christina," Mom continued. "You know he's a good driver. The pickup shoved us sideways, into the ditch. He hit us hard. I'm glad you were asleep when it happened. You were still unconscious when they put you on the stretcher."

"If this is what happened to me," I thought, "What about Steven?" He had been on my lap.

"How bad was Steven hurt, Mom?" I asked.

Mom looked down at the floor and did not answer. Why wouldn't she tell me? Something had to be wrong!

I stared at her, waiting.

"When the truck hit the car, your door was smashed in."

She was stalling. "Mom, what happened?" I insisted.

"There's no easy way to tell you, Christy." Dad began. "Steven was hit pretty hard. On the head. He's here in the hospital being taken care of. Dr. Honey said a bump on the head can do strange things sometimes. Steven has a concussion. Right now he's relying on a machine to keep his body functioning." Dad was silent for a few seconds and then he continued. "Steven has slipped into a coma, honey. The doctors tell us he has a good chance of recovery."

My dad was more serious than I had ever seen him.

"Oh Dad," I looked into his eyes, "Why couldn't this be one of your silly jokes?"

I had held back the tears. I promised myself I would not cry.

My head was spinning! "Why had this happened to Steven? He was only five years old!" were my only thoughts. He meant so much to me. Steven and I had always been so close! We had called each other "Darling" ever since he was old enough to talk.

It didn't occur to me until much later that I was more concerned about my little brother's condition than I was about my own.

"Who was driving that pickup, Dad? Who did this to us?"

Again my father hesitated. "Well Christina, the plot thickens. I'm afraid you are in for a lot of publicity. We were hit by none other than Hubert Bumgardner. You know, the big fat guy who always wears a light blue suit and looks like a used care salesman?"

"Dad, are you kidding? Do you mean the candidate for mayor of Lost Lake?" It couldn't be true!

"Old Hubert, himself, drunker than a skunk!" Dad laughed. "I wasn't going to vote for him anyway and now I'm going to do everything I can to keep him from winning this election."

"Well, isn't he going to jail anyway?" I asked

angrily.

Dad answered, "Probably not. Because he's who he is, the cops didn't do anything to him. But it's not over yet. Anyway, I don't want you to think about it. All I want you to think about is getting well."

There were a lot more questions I wanted to ask. However, my head had started to pound and my left leg was aching. I could ask only one more thing.

"Is Steven going to live?"

Silence.

A nurse came through the door. Mom and Dad looked relieved. They escaped answering.

"Hello!" The petite woman introduced herself, "My name in Anna."

I recognized her as the one who had walked by earlier. She shook hands with my parents and turned to me.

"Hello, Christina. I'm your nurse."

I gave her a weak smile. "Hi."

"The doctor said you would be here about two weeks," Mom informed me, changing the subject. "They have to keep you in traction. Your thigh bone is broken. The bone has to be pulled straight. That's what the traction is doing. At the end of two weeks you'll have surgery. Some pins will be put in,to take the place of the traction. It sounds awful but it's true."

"Why do they have to keep pulling it?" I asked, but before she could answer, I said, "There are stitches in my leg. Did the bone come through the skin?" I had heard about people whose bones had just popped right out. It happened to Gary, a friend of mine, when he had his skiing accident.

"It sure did, honey. You lost a lot of blood because of it."

"Gross," I made a face.

"Do you remember anything about the accident?" Mom questioned.

"I don't remember much. I do remember lying on the stretcher and the lights from the police cars." There was more I wanted to tell them, but not now. I was pretty sure they knew I had died. That news must have really hurt them. What a shock it must have been, finding out I had come to life again. I wanted to tell them about dying and my experience, soon.

Mom and Dad looked disappointed that I didn't remember more, but I really wasn't ready to tell them all that I remembered.

"We're going to go now, Christina, to let you rest. We promised the nurse we wouldn't stay too long tonight." Dad looked at his watch. I knew it had been a stressful day for both of them.

"Have you guys been driving our car?" I asked.

" 'fraid not!" Dad laughed. "Our car went to the hospital too."

"We're driving your dad's old pickup," Mom told me.

They both gave me a kiss and a promise to see me tomorrow.

Anna closed the door behind them. We kept up a pleasant conversation as she checked my pulse and removed the IV from my arm. I was glad to get rid of the needle!

"You're going to be here for two weeks. I guess you knew that already," she smiled. "We should get to be friends."

"I don't really know too much about the accident. I understand you took the worst of it. But, if you're wondering about what you'll be doing here, I can tell you all about that. Is there anything you want, or want to know?"

I wasn't in the mood for talking, but there were things I wanted to know.

"Who's behind that curtain?" I asked.

"Oh, that's Samantha." Anna lowered her voice. "She's been here for a few days, with a kidney problem. But, she'll be going home tomorrow evening.

How would you like that side of the room when she leaves? There's a window over there. Of course, there isn't much to see. After all, we are on the sixth floor. You'll be getting a new roommate soon. Beds don't stay empty around here for very long."

"Oh." I had to smile as I watched her lightly step around the room. The blond curls on the top of her head bounced and fell helplessly on her rosy cheeks. I knew right away that I liked her.

Anna told me that it was too late to make a selection from the dinner menus. She said she had ordered me something from the kitchen and hoped I would not be disappointed.

I remembered when my sister, Sara, was in the hospital. Her favorite part was getting to choose what she wanted from the menus. She always ordered extra desserts. As for me, food was the furthest thing from my mind.

When the tray arrived, something smelled good. Anna showed me how to work the controls to lower and raise my head.

"Make sure you don't move your legs," she told me. "But you can adjust the upper half for comfort anytime you like."

The dinner tray was on a table that swung over my lap. I was unable to sit all the way up because everything hurt! But, I didn't complain. When Anna offered to help me with the food, I told her I would manage.

I ate with my right hand, thankful that it hadn't been injured too. The food wasn't bad. In fact, the chicken soup was great! The sandwich and fruit salad weren't bad either. I ate fast. Then I thought about how long it had been since I had eaten anything. No wonder I was hungry!

Anna told me that while I stayed in traction she would help me do some "fun" exercises to keep my joints from stiffening up. She also told me that Dr. Honey would be in to visit me each morning and evening.

It sounded as if I was in for a lot of boredom!

About six-thirty, Dr. Honey came in. He checked the apparatus on my leg and looked at my stitches. He said if I wanted anything for pain, all I had to do was tell my nurse. He wanted me to rest and be as comfortable as possible. He told me I was young and would heal quickly.

A few minutes before seven, Anna came in to show me how to buzz for a nurse if I needed anything.

"Don't be afraid to use this if you need to. I'm going off duty now. Mrs. Henderson will be your nurse." Then she said good-bye and left the room.

As I lay there, I could see the sunlight peeking around the corners of the curtain that divided the room.

The pain killers I'd been given in surgery were beginning to wear off. My leg hurt so badly I wanted to cry. But my thoughts of Steven were even more painful. Mom and Dad had purposely avoided answering my question when I asked them if Steven was going to die.

"When will I know the truth?" I wondered. "Will I ever again hear his sweet little voice calling me 'Darling'?"

Chapter 5

Tuesday morning, I woke up to the sound of familiar voices. Two women bustled around the room with fresh sheets and towels. The curtain in the middle of the room was pulled back. Samantha still slept. She was a plump, older lady with tight gray curls. Beyond her, I saw the early morning sun shining through the window. It gave a fresh, bright look to everything in the room. I could almost feel the cool morning air.

The hallway was alive with busy people. I watched them pass outside the open door. One nurse brought breakfast. As I ate the eggs, bacon, toast and orange juice, I listened to the conversations around me. I gathered that everyone got most of their work done in the morning.

30

When Samantha woke up, we introduced ourselves. She ate her breakfast and talked to the nurses in a routine-like manner. I figured she was a friendly person. I didn't find out for sure until the nurses left.

"Is it always like this in the morning?" I turned to her with a smile.

"It sure is. You'll get used to it,"she said, straightening her blankets. "As for me, this is my last day here."

"Anna said you were leaving today."

"Yes," she returned. "I'm so excited about going home! Not that you don't get treated well around here or anything like that, but I miss my own bed." She smiled, making the dimples in her round, friendly face grow deeper.

"Oh, you are really going to love Anna," she continued. "She's just the sweetest thing! There's nothing she wouldn't do for you. If you ever get sad or lonely, you know you can always talk to her."

As soon as Samantha had said this, I wanted to get to know Anna as well as she did.

"So, how long are you going to be here? Do you know yet?" She asked.

"Yes, two weeks. Do you think it will be boring?"

She thought for a minute. "Well, I haven't been in

traction, so I don't know anything about that. But, I
do know they'll try to keep you as comfortable and
happy as they can. You can always watch television,
--- or talk with your roommate."

What she meant was, "Yes you are going to be
bored out of your mind!" Perhaps for Samantha,
watching television and visiting had been enough, but
not for me! I knew she was trying to be nice by not
worrying me.

Dr. Honey strode through the door. "Good morning! Hello Samantha. Hello Christina, how was your
night? Any trouble?"

"Mrs. Henderson checked on me several times and
gave me some aspirin. I was all right." Actually, it had
been a terrible night. I woke up often, feeling nau-
seous. My "tractioned" leg had never stopped its'
deep throbbing. But, I had heard that a lot of the
pain killers used in hospitals were addictive. I was
going to do everything I could to stay away from
drugs, even if it meant putting up with a lot of pain.
Maybe I was being foolish, but I didn't think so.

A nurse came in and handed Dr. Honey the clipboard that hung on the foot of my bed. I assumed
it was my record.

"You've only had aspirin, Christina? I know that
leg is hurting you. Wouldn't you like to have something stronger to take that pain away?" he asked.

"No. I'm fine. I don't need anything," I told him.

"All right," he said. I think he was surprised by my answer. "I'll see you girls tonight," he announced and then looked at me. "If you need anything, just holler, O.K.?"

I nodded.

"Samantha will show you the ropes," he laughed. "Bye!"

Samantha turned on the television with a remote control. There wasn't much on at six-thirty . We finally settled on an early morning talk show.

The morning dragged on. We watched game shows and a million commercials. At eleven o'clock, Anna came in.

"Hello, you two. Christina, you are never going to believe what's going on downstairs!"

"What is it?" I hadn't the faintest idea.

"There are a *lot* of reporters down there! They want to see you!"

"Oh, no. Why did Hubert Bumgardner have to pick us to hit?" I said.

"Dr. Honey got rid of them when they came yesterday. But, now they're back again. Dr. Honey said it's up to you, if you want to talk to them or not. What do you think?"

I definately did not feel up to it. It was a hard decision. If I did talk to them, everyone in Lost Lake, and who knows where else, would know about the accident. How embarrassing! But if I did talk, people would find out what Old Hubert had done to us. Maybe then he would lose the election. Better still, he might get thrown in jail where drunk drivers belong!

"Yes, I will talk to them," I told her.

"Good! I was hoping you'd say that," Anna grinned. "This will be so exciting!"

"Exciting" was not the word that came to my mind. In my opinion, a better word was "revenge".

Chapter 6

Visiting hours began at twelve noon. While I waited, I ate lunch and combed my thick red hair. When I raised my arm to comb my hair, I was surprised that the stitches in it didn't hurt. Even though I made my hair look presentable, there was no hiding my leg. I tried covering it with a sheet, but that only made the situation worse. It also made me angrier! With every pang of discomfort, every twinge of embarrassment, and every cutting thought of Stevie, rage grew inside me!

"I'll show that Hubert Bumgardner," I thought, "No one could get away with doing something like this to us." He'd have to pay.

A few minutes before twelve o'clock, Mom and Dad walked in. Dr. Honey had been preparing me for the interview with the reporters.

"I was just telling Christina," he looked at my parents who stood on the right of my bed, "that these news people can be tough customers. I know you both gave permission for them to talk to her, but keep in mind that you are in charge. Don't let them overstep their bounds. If one asks a question that you don't like, then don't answer it."

"We understand," Dad said.

Dr. Honey sounded as though he had dealt with the media before. "Remember, it's no trouble getting them out of here. All right?"

I smiled. "Don't worry!" But, I wasn't as brave as I sounded!

Dr. Honey sent Anna to bring the reporters up when visiting hours began. Anxiously, Mom, Dad, Samantha and I waited for them to arrive. I couldn't understand why I felt so nervous. So many times I had been up on a stage, singing for a full house, and had never been nervous. Maybe the fact that those performances had been rehearsed, made a difference. With the reporters, ---what if I said the wrong thing?

The minutes we waited seemed like hours. Finally, about a dozen reporters filed through the door. They snapped pictures while positioning themselves between the two beds. Now I knew what an animal in the zoo felt like!

Dr. Honey explained that the questions were to be asked in an orderly fashion and said that the patient was not to be upset.

I was glad my parents and Dr. Honey stood by my side.

As soon as the red lights on the television cameras came on, my leg started aching. A lot! I prayed no one could see the pain I was feeling.

Dr. Honey knew.

"Christina, just this once, won't you please take something to help with the pain? You'll get through this easier," he offered kindly. But I refused.

The questioning commenced, with the obvious question.

"How are you feeling today?" someone asked.

I surprised myself when I answered. "Not too great."

Dr. Honey told me that the fellow who had asked was Keith Ryan, from the Evening Banner.

"The policeman who filed the accident report said that Hubert Bumgardner was the one who crashed into your car. How do you feel about that, Christina? Did you see anything?" This time I recognized the speaker as Allison Farnes from Channel 16.

"No, I didn't see anything. I was asleep in the

back seat. You'll have to ask my parents about that."

"Bumgardner had been drinking," my dad said. "When he got out of his car, he even fell down on the pavement! Have you talked to him? The last time we saw him, he was being taken away in a police car, but, we understand no arrest was made."

"He hasn't been available for comment," Allison told us.

"I'll just bet he hasn't," Dad laughed.

"I can't believe he was drinking and driving," my mother offered. "He spoke at our P.T.A. meeting last week. In fact,he pledged full support to the M.A.D.D. (Mother's Against Drunk Drivers) organization." That statement brought on a frenzy of picture taking.

"Good for you, Mom," I thought.

"How has this affected your family?" Gene Adams, from the Lost Lake Review questioned.

"What a dumb thing to ask!" I thought. "Is he blind?"

"Our other two kids are spending a lot of time at their grandparent's house," Dad smiled.

"Sara and Shawn?" Allison asked.

Mom answered. "Yes. Sara was in the front seat between us when the accident happened.She's twelve. Shawn was in the back seat, ---on the safe side. He's our ten year old."

"Were they wearing seat belts?" Don Ellis from Channel 11 asked.

"We all were," I assured them. "Little good it did us." I raised my head higher, feeling better now.

"I want to know why Hubert Bumgardner got away with hitting us." I asked them. "He was a drunk driver! Why isn't he in jail?" I made sure that I was looking directly into a television camera. "I like this town. The last thing I want to see is a phoney like this guy elected as our mayor." Flashes of light lit up the room.

The next few questions that followed were about me. I told them that after summer, I'd be a sophomore at Thomas High School. Dr. Honey handled the inquiries about my condition.

It was Keith Ryan's statement and questions that broke up the session.

"I know I speak for all of us Christina, when I say we are truly sorry that this incident took place. From what I've seen, you aren't comfortable lying there in that contraption, yet you are a very courageous girl. I haven't heard you complain once. I know that in a couple of weeks you'll be up and walking, but what about Steven?"

I closed my eyes as a crushing sensation weighted upon my chest.

"Your little brother's life is on the line," he continued. "He depends entirely upon a life support system. What if he doesn't make it Christina? What do you think should happen to the man who is responsible for all this?"

Steven, not make it? The thought was more than I could bear. My eyes were blinded with tears. They streamed down my cheeks and splashed on my arms. The pain in my heart was the worst I'd ever known.

"I believe my brother will live," I pushed the words out from behind the tears. "But, if I'm wrong, I hope Bumgardner, ---fries." I meant it.

Mom put her arms around me.

Dr. Honey dismissed them. "That's it." He motioned for them to leave. The room emptied in a matter of seconds. They had gotten more than they'd hoped for.

Mom and Dad sensed that I needed to be alone. Dr. Honey shut the divider curtain and left.

Once he had gone, I tried to sort my feelings out. "This type of thing is only supposed to happen on T.V.," I told myself. "Not to real people!"

I cried myself to sleep.

Chapter 7

A couple hours later, I woke up. Anna was helping Samantha pack her things.

"Well, it's about time," Samantha grinned. "I almost thought you wouldn't wake up in time to say good-bye! I can't wait to tell my friends who my hospital roommate was, Christina."

Anna glanced at the clock above the door. "Your grandparents are coming to see you at three-thirty."

"Really? Will Sara and Shawn be with them?"

'Mmm hmm."

Wow! That was wonderful news! But waiting was not easy. Seeing Sara and Shawn would be fun. Even better than that, I planned to tell Grandma and Grandpa about my death experiences with Great-grandpa. I still hadn't told anyone. It wasn't like me not to tell Mom something as important as that. But, the right moment had not presented itself. Besides, I wanted to tell Grandma first. After all, it was *her* father I had seen.

At three o'clock Anna and I said good-bye to Samantha. A nurse had come with a wheelchair to take her downstairs to her husband.

Anna switched my bed and belongings with Samantha's place, as promised. It was brighter and warmer on the window side. I enjoyed the change.

Three-thirty came around, eventually. Grandma lightly tapped on the door and opened it. She stepped in, followed by a parade of smiling, curious faces. While Grandma and Grandpa gave me a hug, Sara and Shawn explored the room. They worked their way over to us, then examined my leg and the weights at the foot of my bed.

"Hey, Christy," Shawn gave me a sideways smile. "Why is your leg up like that?"

Before I could answer. Sara spotted the metal pin through my leg, below the knee.

"Oh! How gross!" She squealed. "How can you, ---I mean, why, ---Oh, I can't believe it!" She covered her mouth with her hand.

I began to laugh. I laughed so hard my stomach hurt.

"Sara, don't worry. It's not as bad as it looks."

Actually, I thought it was pretty disgusting, too. I'd just never said it out loud, or *as* loud as she did.

"Dr. Honey, that's my doctor Sara, had to put a pin through the bone so that pressure on the bones would keep them in line. If that pin was not there, the broken part wouldn't heal right." I explained, but Sara's and Shawn's confused expressions told me that they didn't quite understand.

"In a couple of weeks," Grandma said, "she'll get a cast and crutches."

"Oh." Shawn understood that part. After a moment of silence, Sara grabbed his hand and pulled him to the T.V. I switched it on with the remote control. Then the cartoons carried them away.

Grandpa took his hand out from behind his back. In it was a present wrapped in shiny pink paper and tied with a silver bow. He smiled a silly smile and set the package in my lap.

"Just a little something to keep you entertained!" Grandpa chuckled.

"Open it while we're here, Christina," Grandma urged. "I want to see how you like it."

I pulled off the ribbon and tore the paper away from the box. When I took the lid off, I saw first a deck of Muggens cards. Underneath the cards lay a neatly folded, button-down-the-front nightgown, made of silky white material with lace trim. When I picked it up for a better look, what I saw in the bottom of the box took me by surprise. I looked down and saw the works, "Le Nozze Di Figaro" stamped in silver letters and knew it was the full opera score of Mozart's, "The Marriage of Figaro". Lifting it gently from the box, I carressed the pages. I could not believe it! My own copy!

"Thank you! Thank you! Thank you!" I breathed the words. It was a treasured gift. I felt so happy, I nearly cried. I'd been singing arias from that opera, but using my voice teacher's book.

"You've wanted your own copy for so long. I thought it might cheer you up," Grandma said.

How right she was. There was a card in the very bottom of the box. I picked it up and looked at the funny picture on the front. Inside it read:

Christina,

> We love you so much! Get well or we'll
>> disinherit you!

Grandma and Grandpa C.

"Hey Christy," Shawn turned from the television long enough to ask me a question. "Can you sing with your leg up in that sling?" He laughed.

"Sure I can." I told him. My family knew that I

loved to sing; anytime and anyplace.

I was anxious to try out my new gift. Quietly, I sang.

"Voi, chesapete che cosae'amor,
Donne, vedete, s'io l'ho nel cor --"

"At least you didn't break your voice, Christy," Sara giggled.

"Thanks, Sara."

We talked for a while about Sara and Shawn staying with them and about Hubert Bumgardner.

They told me they had seen Steven. Grandpa said Steven's condition had not changed and that he looked like he was asleep.

"Grandma, I have to ask you something." I said.

"Yes?"

"Does everyone know that I died?" My question brought a peculiar look to her face.

"You know?" She exclaimed.

"Of course! I've known ever since it happened."

Grandpa and Grandma exchanged glances. "What exactly did happen?" Grandma asked, looking even more puzzled.

"Well, I remember waking up in the emergency room. Several people were working over me. I heard them talking and knew I was dying." Grandma squeezed my hand.

Sara and Shawn began paying attention to what I was saying.

Shawn's eyes grew large and inquiring, "Did it hurt?"

"Did what hurt?" I asked him.

"Dying."

"I really didn't feel anything." I told my brother. "Everything sort of went black. The next thing I knew, I was up near the ceiling looking down on everything."

"Are you makin' this up?" Sara drawled disbelievingly.

"No, I'm totally serious. I could see my body below me and the nurses and doctors working to bring me back to life. I even watched a nurse record my death."

Grandma hung on every word. "I've heard of these things happening to other people, Christina. Were you frightened?"

"Not really. It was a peaceful feeling.I didn't hurt and didn't seem to be broken," I said, remembering the experience. "Everyone left the emergency room, after I had died. They covered my body with a sheet. Then, this shimmering white light surrounded me. When it cleared away, I found myself in a long, dark tunnel. At the end of it I could see a different kind

kind of light, more like sunlight. I walked toward it."

"You mean, you had a body?" Grandma questioned.

I nodded. "I didn't have any injuries either. Now that I think about it, that part was pretty weird. Anyway, I came out of the tunnel into this huge parklike place. There were luscious, green trees and a pond. Birds were singing and the sun was shining bright. It was so beautiful. Remember the time you took us to Canada to Butchart Gardens and how we thought it was the most beautiful place we'd ever seen? This place was even better than that." I went on to tell them about the apple tree and my visit with Great-grandpa. My grandma got a tear in her eye when I told her about her father, and what he had said to me.

"He's just like you said he was, Grandma." I said.

Sara squeeked, "This is really neat stuff!"

Shawn agreed, "It's kinda like a movie I saw once,"

I could just hear those two blabbing to all the neighbors!

They must have stayed for about an hour longer. I answered a lot of questions about my life after death experience. I told them everything I could recall. Before they left, I sang a few more lines of the arietta.

I wondered if I should have told them not to tell anyone about the unusual event I had related to them.

I didn't want anymore run-ins with reporters!

Chapter 8

As I lay there alone, I stared out the window at a blue sky steaked with feathery clouds that moved slowly past my view.

I wondered what I'd be doing at that moment if the accident had never happened. My imagination captured all our neighbors and friends sprawled out in our backyard, eating watermelon. I pictured my dad wearing his, "I love to BBQ" apron, flipping the hot dogs and steaks over the grill. The younger kids would be playing with Bootsie, our beagle. Stevie would be running around with them, having a good time.

"But here we are Stevie, you and me," I thought. Our summer fun had been taken from us. Steven's entire life may have been stolen from him! I had never hated anyone, but I hated Bumgardner!

"Why has this happened to us?" I asked myself over and over. None of it made any sense. We hadn't done anything wrong, but we were being punished.

My thoughts drifted back to a night about a month before. Stevie and I were spending the night at Grandma's and Grandpa's house in the country. It was a particularly warm evening, so we planned to sleep outside.

We were lying on our backs, looking up at the sky. Stevie gazed up into space. I pointed out the big dipper. He'd always been fascinated by the stars.

"Stevie, Darling," I glanced over at him, "don't the stars look close when we're in the country?"

"Oh, yes," he replied. "They're bee-you-tee-ful!"

We were silent until a shooting star blazed across the black sky.

"Oh! Look Darling! Did you see that?" Stevie blurted. I was glad he had seen it.

"Yes, that was a great one, wasn't it? It had such a long tail!"

Stevie had jumped up in excitement. Finally, he lay back down beside me.

"Darling, don't you just love the apples in the sky?" he asked.

"What? Apples in the sky? Do you mean stars?"

I had to laugh.

There was a smile on his face. "That's so cute, Stevie," I giggled.

I don't think he understood why I was laughing, but he joined in, anyway.

"I love you, Darling," He said after we'd quieted down.

"I love you too, Stevie." As I said this, he kissed me on the nose.

My little brother was so sweet. He didn't deserve to be in the condition he was in. I wished that it had been me, instead.

Again, tears streamed down my face. What if he didn't make it?

"Please Stevie," I prayed, "hold on!"

Chapter 9

Now that I was allowed visitors, other than my family, my friends began dropping in. By Thursday, my room was jam packed with flowers and cards!

Mom and Dad came every day. They brought me articles from newspapers and video-recorded television interviews of me. I couldn't believe how the reporters exaggerated! They made my situation sound much more exciting than it really was.

When my friends came to visit, I think they expected to see a lot of glamour and glitz. Actually, the only time I wasn't bored, was when someone came to visit. The rest of the time, I was just plain depressed. Playing solitaire, singing, when I felt up to it, and watching T.V. were poor substitutes for the active life I normally led.

Anna was worried about me. The promised new roommate never materialized. I imagined the hospital was concerned about putting anyone else in my room because of all the publicity. I knew Anna felt sorry for me. She was a kind, caring person. Once, she mentioned that she thought a fourteen year old being cooped up all day was unhealthy.

I tried to look happy whenever she came in, but Anna could see right through my disguise. On Friday morning, she did something about it.

As I sat up in bed, staring down at an aria I planned to learn, Anna pushed the door open. Immediately, my eyes turned to her, noticing her triumphant expression. She quickly glided over to me.

"I want you to meet someone."

"Who?" I asked, hoping it wasn't a famous reporter or something.

Without answering, she chimed, "I can't believe I never thought of it before! Oh you're going to love me for this." A second later, Anna was opening the door and motioning to someone in the hall. Then she announced, "This is Adam Jacobs, my brother and sometimes, my friend."

A blond guy about my age walked into the room. He must have been at least six feet tall. He smiled a handsome smile politely, as if to say, "Sorry, this wasn't my idea."

Anna introduced us. I sure didn't mind being introduced to a person as cute as he was, but at the same time, I couldn't stop thinking, "Oh Anna, what have you gotten me into?"

"Adam works here at the hospital." Anna watched us both, not knowing how awkward we felt. "Since you are alone a lot, I thought you needed someone to talk to. I've told him about you. I know you two will have much to talk about. You have many things in common."

Dr. Honey opened the door, " There you are, Anna! Can I borrow you for a minute?"

"I'll be right there." She started out, telling us to get acquainted and have fun.

"I didn't know Anna had a brother," I said when she'd gone.

"Well, actually she has six."

"Oh my gosh! Are you serious?" I thought that my two brothers were plenty!

"Yes. There's me, and Alex, and Andrew, and Aaron, and Alvin, and Arnie, and then the girls, Adrian, Aerial, and Andrea. In that order."

"I take it your parents liked 'A' names," I laughed.

"Yeah, Mom calls us the 'A' team."

He pulled up a chair. "While I'm here, I might as well stay. Anna usually gets her way," he laughed.

I could tell Adam really liked his sister. How could he help it?

"So, you're the 'miracle' girl? He grinned.

"Oh, no! I bet everyone in Lost Lake saw that!" I could feel my cheeks get warm, remembering the article in the Lost Lake Examiner.

"I think it's pretty cool. You're lucky." Adam was beginning to feel more at ease. What he said made me think about how "unlucky" Steven was.

"So, what do you do here?" I changed the subject.

"Well, I sweep up, sometimes I bring the doctors coffee, but I'm basically the gopher for the first eight floors."

"Sounds exciting!" I joked.

"Well, anything to save money, I'm going to be an exchange student my junior year."

"Really? So am I! Where are you going?"

"New Zealand," he answered.

"Wow, how fun! I am saving ---, was saving to go to Austria." That was another thing that made me angry. There would be no more babysitting and odd jobs for me this summer. Very little is available to a fourteen year old, but I always managed to find work. I wondered how long my recovery would take.

After that, Adam and I talked non-stop about school and our exchange student plans. He told me he was fifteen. We did have a lot in common. He would be going to Thomas High, too. We both enjoyed a strange combination of Mozart and the "Escape Clubs" music.

I couldn't believe it! I had a great time. Adam was so funny and easy to be with. When Anna came to remind him that his lunch-break was almost over, I was sorry he had to leave.

"Adam, time's up," Anna called from the doorway and then disappeared.

"I'd better go." He got up reluctantly. "I'll come back to talk to you soon." We had been acting like we'd known each other forever. I think he remembered that we had just met. "If that's O.K. with you, I mean." He smiled.

"Sure. This has been fun." I meant it.

Adam headed for the door.

"Thank you." I said.

"I should thank you!" He tipped an invisible hat and with a twirl of his hand, bowed. "Goodbye," his blue eyes smiled.

"See you soon."

"Maybe now I won't be so lonely. After all, he

said he'd be back. And, he *was* cute," I thought. His visit had been fun. Already, I looked forward to seeing him again.

Then, guilt set in. How could I make new friends and feel happy when Stevie, ---

Suddenly, I felt very selfish.

Chapter 10

Adam came to see me the next day and the next. Each time, we talked and laughed. Time flew by when he was there. I had liked other boys, but the way I liked Adam, was different.

Anna was as pleased as punch! She was so happy that she'd come up with the idea of Adam keeping me company.

I enjoyed Adam's visits. Maybe I enjoyed them too much. I felt so guilty, but I didn't want to stop being friends with him.

Tuesday afternoon, I marked the calendar. Dr. Honey had set my surgery for July 2nd. Only five days away! As strange as it seemed, I couldn't wait. After surgery, I'd be able to walk. And, I'd be able to see Stevie.

At three o'clock, Anna rushed into my room, breathless.

"There are reporters downstairs again. They're on their way up!"

"What? Tell them to leave!" The last thing I wanted was to deal with more reporters.

"It's too late! Guess who's with them. Hubert Bumgardner!" Anna was excited.

"What? Bumgardner? Can't you stop them? What does he want?"

"We're trying to locate Dr. Honey. He'll ---" Anna was cut short.

The door swung open. First Bumgardner's beer-belly appeared, and then Bumgardner. He waddled over to us, followed by a stampede of reporters.

"Aw, honey. Poor little thing!" His high voice whined.

Anna backed the reporters off.

"I'm real, real sorry. And, I'm so ashamed!" Bumgardner put his hand over his eyes.

How phoney! I couldn't believe what was happening.

"I jus' came to say I am so sorry." He looked at the reporters with a pitiful expression, then turned to me. "Can ye ever forgive a man for makin' a bad mistake?"

I stared at him in disgust. He expected me to forgive him? And right here in front of these television cameras, too! I'll bet he didn't expect what I said next!

"Who do you think you are, barging in like this? How can you be so heartless? You expect me to forgive you? You big phoney! I can see right through this little publicity game you're playing!" I was practically screaming now. The reporters took pictures like crazy.

"If you think saying 'sorry' will solve everything, you are wrong! You can't get away with what you've done! Drinking and driving is against the law, no matter who you are! I'll never forgive you for what you've done to my little brother and me! You bumbling idiot!" Now I screamed at the top of my lungs! "Get out of here!"

It sure was effective! As soon as I had said that, a stunned Bumgardner turned and hurried out the door.

Anna shooed the reporters out behind him. Most of them were smiling. They had their story, but it wasn't the one Bumgardner had anticipated. His little stunt had backfired!

Dr. Honey came in a few minutes later to apologize for Bumgardner getting in.

Anna assured him, "Don't worry. This girl can take care of herself! Don't ever underestimate the temper of a redhead! Especially, this redhead!"

Dr. Honey just happened to be in my room when the eight o'clock news came on. We watched the whole scene.

"I see what Anna meant!" he laughed

I hoped I had seen the last of Bumgardner, and reporters.

Chapter 11

Dr. Honey gave me the usual check-up Wednesday morning. He said that the exercises Anna had been helping me do were working. At least my joints hadn't stiffened up. He told me that things would go exactly as planned, and my surgery would be Monday morning.

What good news! Not only would I be able to walk, but at last I could see Steven. Great-grandpa had said Steven needed my help. I thought if I could see him and talk to him, maybe I could do some good. No brother and sister could be closer than Steven and I. If anyone were to reach him, that someone would be me. In that, I felt confident.

My day began perfectly. Grandma and Grandpa dropped by with Sara and Shawn. They told me their plans to take Sara, Shawn and me to the beach for a week-end when my hospital stay was over.

Mom and Dad came in to tell me about the re-decorating they'd done in the room Sara and I shared. They hoped I would like it. I hoped I would too! I knew what my parents were doing. They were keeping busy, trying to keep their minds off of Stevie and me. Mostly Stevie.

Also, they gave me the latest news about Bumgardner. All the bad publicity had brought his campaign to a crawl. His campaign workers were walking out by the dozens.

I hadn't realized how hard my parents had been fighting against Bumgardner. They had the backing of drunk driving victims and their families, who were finally taking a stand. Bumgardner's chances of becoming mayor were very slim.

Things seemed to be going beautifully, but little did I know. It was mid-afternoon when someone tapped me on the shoulder. Mom was back. She woke me up from a nap. With her were Anna and Dr. Honey. They looked serious! Mom looked as if she had been crying.

Anna picked up my remote to put me in a sitting position.

"What's wrong? Has something happened to

Steven?" I asked, Steven always being the first thing on my mind.

"No, that's what we've come to talk to you about," Dr. Honey said sadly. "I know you don't want to hear what I'm going to tell you, but a decision has to be made. Steven is no better off than the day he was admitted to the hospital. We've had the best specialists here for your brother. We've kept him on life support, monitoring every minute. We've done all we can do."

"What are you trying to say?" I snapped.

"What I'm trying to say is that everyone who has been involved with Steven's care, agrees that his chances of ever recovering are one in a million. There is nothing more we can do. We could keep him here on life support for the rest of his life and rely on that one chance, or we can discontinue his life support and it would all be done."

"All be done?" A lump was in my throat. "I thought you said he would recover."

"I'm sorry. We were hopeful, but a condition like Steven's can be extremely complicated," Dr. Honey said.

I looked at them with tears in my eyes. "Is that what you want? Is that what you've come to tell me? Where is your faith?"

I could see how painful this was for my mother, but she tried to reason with me.

"We only want what's best. There's no reason to keep him alive if he'll always be the way he is now."

"Mom, I thought you would be against all of this."

"Christina," Dr. Honey said quietly, "hospital bills for comatose patients are astronomical. Your parents will be financially drained, year after year, and it will never do Steven any good. It will only burdon your family."

"But what if he does wake up? Soon. Would he be normal?" I questioned.

Dr. Honey answered thoughtfully, "He's not brain dead, so yes he would be normal, but ---"

"So if he wakes up he'll be fine!" I paused. "Just give me a chance to see him, speak to him, I know if you only gave me the chance I could, ---. Please wait until I'm able to go in there to see him."

Mom and Dr. Honey glanced at each other.

"Mom, don't you see? Don't you understand? He's your son! A one in a million chance is better than none."

"You're being unreasonable." Dr. Honey said to me. "I know this is quite a shock for you, but we have to face the facts."

I looked directly at my mother. "It's a matter of

faith," I told them simply.

"Doctor," Mom touched his arm. "Let's wait for another week or so."

Dr. Honey sighed. I had won!

"Oh, thank you!" I cried, hoping that I had bought myself enough time!

Chapter 12

Adam came in to see me after work.

"Hey! Cheer up!" He laughed as he walked towards me.

I managed to smile.

"That's better. Anna told me about Steven. She said you talked Dr. Honey out of it. She also said if anyone could do it, you could."

I nodded.

"Well then, what's the gloomy face for?"

"I just don't know if I have enough time, or if Steven has enough ---" Without warning, silent tears streamed down my face. I wiped them from my eyes.

"I'm sorry. I just can't bear to think of it."

Adam gently touched my shoulder. "Don't worry." he said softly, "I wish I could promise you that everything will be fine. I really do."

Somehow his words made me feel better.

I could hear Anna's voice in the hall.

"Anna's going to give me a ride home tonight." He looked at his watch. "I have to go."

"Bye." He left me alone with my thoughts.

I hadn't wanted him to leave. That was what really bothered me. I had never felt about someone the way I felt about Adam. I thought about him more than I meant to. His visits were special. When I heard anyone coming, I secretly hoped it was him. He made me happy. I felt selfish and tormented by my feelings for him. I had no right to feel happy about anything! It wasn't fair to Steven for me to have glad feelings when he couldn't feel anything at all.

After thinking it over again and again, I knew there was only one thing to do.

The next morning Anna brought me breakfast.

"Anna?" I said.

"Yes?"

"I don't really know how to say this. I mean --- Well it was so nice of you to introduce me to Adam. He has been a great friend and a lot of company. But -------"

"But what?" she asked, concerned.

"Um. What I'm trying to say is, well, does he

mind coming in to talk to me and stuff?"

"No! Not at all! I'm not holding a gun to his head, if that's what you mean."

"Oh, why couldn't I just say it?" I thought.

"Anna," I said hesitantly, "What I wanted to ask was," I stopped and then blurted, "could you please ask him not to come to see me anymore?"

Boy! That took her by surprise!

"Christina, I was under the impression you two really liked each other." Anna searched my face for an answer, but there was no answer to be found. Not one that she could understand anyway.

"Anna, could you just do that for me?"

After a long minute of silence, she said, "If that's what you want." She left quickly with a blank look on her face.

"Oh, no!" I sighed. "Now they'll both be mad at me. What have you done this time, Christina?"

Then I reminded myself of the reason I had come to that decision. I thought of Steven in that hospital bed. "No," I decided. "I am doing the right thing."

I made up my mind that I would try to forget everything except Steven. All my thoughts and energy would be devoted to him.

For the next few days, I did exactly what I had planned. By the time Sunday came around, I was a nervous wreck. It was hopeless! I hadn't come up with even one idea of how to help Steven recover.

Mom and Dad were worried when they visited me Sunday night.

"Are you sure you aren't nervous about the surgery, hon?" Mom asked.

"Positive. I'm just excited." Actually, I was anxious to get the surgery over with and be able to walk, but I was scared, too.

"Relax, babe!" Dad laughed.

"Listen, don't worry about me you guys. I'm fine."

"We just don't want *you* to worry. Dr. Honey will take good care of you." Mom sounded more concerned than I did, even though she tried to hide it. I knew my surgery was neither complicated nor life threatening, but mothers are worriers.

"We'll all be here around seven o'clock in the morning. All right?" Dad reminded me.

"O.K. How long do you think my surgery will take?"

"Dr. Honey didn't know for sure. "I would guess a couple of hours," Dad said.

I was thankful that I would be asleep while they worked on me.

Mom smiled. "You'll be coming home Tuesday

morning, Christina."

"Hooray!" I thought.

Anna walked in. Ever since I'd asked her to tell Adam not to visit me anymore, she'd been acting strange. Kind of distant. It was no wonder. What I had done was terrible. Adam must have been totally mystified. I should have offered an explanation. Even so, I kept trying to convince myself that I'd done the right thing.

"So, tomorrow's the big day," Anna said cheerfully.

"It sure is!" I returned Anna's smile, trying to be friendly.

"Christy, I can't believe we almost forgot to tell you." Dad grinned. "Our old friend Bumgardner is in trouble again. First of all, when it hit the papers that Steven probably won't recover, Bumgardner's campaign all but folded. There's no way he'll ever become mayor."

"Thank goodness!" I breathed a sigh of relief. But, I knew in my heart that Steven *would* recover.

"That's not the half of it! Last night, some news team followed Bumgardner to a bar. About midnight, they filmed him coming out to his car. One of the news guys told him not to drive. Bumgardner was so drunk, he just ignored him. Then, the reporters threatened to call the police if he got into his car. Well, Bumgardner got into his car laughing. He told them to go ahead and call, it wouldn't do any good. Then he spilled the beans about how he'd bribed the police before, and he could do it again. What do you think of that? They got it all on camera!"

"Oh my gosh! Dad this is wonderful!" I was about to burst with happiness.

"You'll see it tonight on the news."

"This is like a dream come true!" For a moment I forgot about Steven. His waking up was the dream I really wanted to come true.

"We did it." Dad said. "We got justice. When everyone in Lost Lake hears Bumgardner on T.V. tonight, putting his foot in his mouth, the police will have to take care of him, no matter how much money he has, or who he's paid off. Bumgardner will finally get what he deserves. I'm sure of that!"

Just then my friend Teague bounced through the door, followed by Matt, Laura, Heather, Joy, Danita, Gary, my sister Sara, and Jenny. I wondered how they all got up there at the same time without being stopped. Immediately, the room was filled with laughter and greetings.

"We just came to wish you luck," Jenny said.

Matt yelled over the commotion, "Wanna hear a

new joke about this man who goes in for an operation and the doctor accidently removes his ----"

"Matt! Don't you dare!" Laura shoved him. "Grow up!"

"Nose! What did you think I was going to say?" Matt teased.

So many people were talking at once! I had to quiet them down. "One at a time! Everyone stop!"

They all laughed. It would be impossible for this group to get together and be quiet.

"Hey McDade," Teague said, "You're quite the celebrity."

"Oh, yes, I'm so popular!" I joked.

"Is that pretty uncomfortable?" Laura asked. She hadn't visited me before and had never seen a person in traction.

"I'm getting used to it. ------Matt!" I yelled! Matt was tickling the bottom of my "tractioned" foot.

"Matt! Stop that!" Somebody pushed him away.

"Thanks for coming," I said to them all.

"No problem. See, I told you guys she'd love my wonderful idea," Joy laughed.

"Oh, Joy!" Jenny said. "It was Teague's idea. She called us all and asked us to come here."

"Teague, my ever-faithful friend!" I dramatically kidded.

"Yes, McDade. I thought you would like a farewell party."

"It was nice knowing you." Heather faked tears.

"Oh, please spare me!" I smiled.

They all shoved get well cards at me. I opened them up, one by one, as each giver looked on.

"You better hurry up and get well," Jenny giggled. "The sale at the Clothes Factory is almost over!"

"Christina, you're not going to believe this! Yesterday, when Joy and I were at the mall, right in front of the Clothes Factory, we saw Jeanette Freedman with Randy Parks. They must be going out or something." Heather usually filled me in on the lastest who's-going-out-with-whom gossip.

Everyone joined in, telling me the latest news about themselves and my other friends. Normally, I would have been interested, but I felt so far removed from those things now.

When visiting hours were over, my friends left. They sounded like a stampede as they goodbyed me and tromped out.

My crazy companions had made me feel better. But, they'd gotten me thinking. I had always been interested in the latest sale at the mall or what couples were going out and breaking up. It was different now. Nothing mattered to me except Stevie. He was what really counted.

"What if something goes wrong with the surgery?" I wondered. "What if I won't be able to walk for a long time? And what about Stevie? They could pull the plug on him and I would never know it." I drove myself bonkers thinking about everything that could go wrong.

Chapter 13

(Monday Morning)

At seven o'clock, Mom and Dad showed up with Sara, Shawn, and Grandma and Grandpa as planned.

Dr. Honey had explained the procedures for the morning to me the night before, so I knew that I would skip breakfast, go into surgery at seven-thirty and be taken back to my room as soon as the effects of the Sodium Pentothal had worn off.

My family planned to stay until the surgery was over. They wanted to know as soon as possible how it went and if I was O.K.

Just after we had said a family prayer in my room, Dr. Honey came in.

"So, are you ready?" he asked.

"I guess I'm as ready as I'll every be." I answered

nervously.

My stomach growled loudly, bringing laughter from everyone.

"We can't let you have any food or drink before surgery. But don't worry, you'll get a big lunch," Dr. Honey smiled.

Dad suggested that they all go down to the cafeteria for breakfast and to wait.

"How dare you say that in front of a starving person!" I laughed.

One by one, they gave me hugs and told me not to worry. I felt like I was going on vacation, all by myself!

Anna brought in the I.V. I hated the needle! She stuck it into my arm trying to be gentle, but it hurt just the same. Ouch!

After that, I didn't remember much, except for feeling kind of dizzy. Once, I looked at the clock. It was seven-twenty-two. I remembered Dr. Honey saying something like, "She's ready to go down to surgery now." Then I went to la-la land.

The next thing I knew, Anna was shaking my arm.

"Come on, wake up now. You've got to wake up."

Boy, this sounded familiar.

I didn't try to speak right away, because I recalled the way my words had gotten stuck in my mouth the last time I had been in that condition.

"Stay awake, Christina. Wake up and smell the roses," Anna said, nodding toward a new bouquet of red roses on the stand by my bed. Anna continued her coaxing.

"Wake up, Christina. Look at you leg. It isn't swinging in the air anymore."

That did it! I was anxious to see what they had done to me. When I attempted to look down at it, my head spun. I pushed the button that raised me up.

Anna watched. "Wow, this is a quick recovery!"

I grinned at her and then looked at my leg. It was in a long blue cast. The kind made out of foam rubbery type stuff.

The new sight took me by surprise. For two weeks I had been staring at my left leg in a sling!

The leg was propped up on a pillow. Even though my whole body felt kind of tingly and numb, I knew by the dull soreness in my hip and leg that I was in for some pain.

Nevertheless, seeing my new freedom was nothing less than katureferpeango! This was my grandpa's own word, meaning "too wonderful for words." It's pronounced ka-tour'-ee-fer-pee-ango.

"Everything went fine," Anna said.

Dr. Honey strode over to us. "Well, I just put another successful surgery notch on my stethoscope! How do you feel, Christina?"

"Thirsty!"

Anna handed me a glass of water. I gulped it down.

"I would advise you not to go near any strong magnets," Dr. Honey laughed. "That left leg is so full of pins, you could build a cadillac with all the metal in there!"

"Ha Ha. Very funny." I smirked.

"Do you want some lunch now?" Anna questioned.

"Sure. I'm starved!" I exclaimed. "How come I feel so good? Shouldn't I be in pain?"

Dr. Honey grinned. "We tricked you this time, Christina. We knew you would never agree to taking a pain killer, so, we gave you something while you were asleep. You'll be quite comfortable for a few hours."

My family came in for a few minutes to see for themselves that I was all right. They wanted to know who the roses were from. I asked Anna. She said she wasn't in the room when they arrived. There was no card. How strange!

"Oh, Christy! Roses? No card? Sounds suspicious!" Sara teased.

I didn't tell Sara, but I had a pretty good idea who the flowers were from.

When the food arrived, my family left. I ate slowly in silence, every bite tasted good.

"Anna," I said, when she came for my tray, "I'll be able to see Stevie today, right?"

"Yes. If you feel up to it. We can take you to him in a wheelchair. Dr. Honey dcesn't want you on crutches today. But he knew that one way or the other, you would want to see Steven."

"A wheelchair is fine with me. Can we go now?" I was anxious.

"I talked to your parents, Christina. They want to be here when you see Steven, They'll be back about noon. So, why don't you get some rest."

Reluctantly, I agreed to wait. Anna lowered my head, hoping I would rest. I tried, but it was impossible. I thought of nothing but Steven. I realized that I was running out of time.

Chapter 14

When twelve o'clock came, so did my parents. I hadn't slept a wink.

"Listen to that wind!" Dad said as he walked in.

"Is is cold out there?" I asked.

"It was about eighty-five degrees until about ten minutes ago." Mom told me. "Now it feels like sixty outside."

"Yeah, looks like we're in for a storm," Dad offered. "I haven't heard the weather report, but I would imagine they're predicting thunder and lightning."

Dr. Honey pushed a wheelchair into the room. I thought that was strange. The orderlies usually got those jobs.

I had to laugh at Dr. Honey, since he was always

teasing me. "Where's all your slave labor today?" I joked.

He grinned.

"Do you think you are up to this, Christina?" I think Dr. Honey knew the answer.

"Of course. I've been waiting for this for two weeks. Nothing will stop me now."

"Even pain?" He gave me a knowing look.

"How does he do that?" I thought. "How does he always know when I am in pain?"

"Even pain," I retorted matter-of-factly.

Dad started toward the door. "Well, are we ready?"

"I am!" I slid to the edge of my bed. Dr. Honey wheeled the chair to me. He and Dad helped me into it. Getting in the chair make my leg hurt worse, but I wasn't about to show it. I gave Dr. Honey a triumphant look.

"Before we go, I have to tell you that this won't be easy. We've talked about this before, Christina, ---" Dr. Honey began.

I interrupted, "You guys don't worry about me. I've thought about this a lot. I will be fine."

Dad pushed me and the wheelchair out the door. I had always wondered what the rest of the hospital looked like. The only part I'd seen was my room.

We went down the hall, passing seven doors. Dad stopped in front of the eighth while Dr. Honey opened it.

I closed my eyes and held my breath for an instant. Maybe I wasn't as brave as I thought I was. What I saw make my heart pound. My sweet little brother, lying there on the hospital bed. He appeared to be asleep.

The room was too quiet; it was like a morgue. Steven was alone.

There was a tube that ran across his upper lip. I figured it had something to do with his breathing. Even with the machines all around him and that tube, he still looked rather peaceful. I expected to see much worse, but he didn't look any different than he had before.

No one said a word, I could see they were waiting for my reaction.

I noticed the T.V. on the wall like in my own room.

"Mom," I said, "Could you please turn on some cartoons?"

She turned her puzzled face to me and without question, turned on Stevie's favorite channel. "Bugs Bunny" was on.

I did not explain my request. My reasoning was

that if Stevie was going to wake up, it would take familiar sounds to bring him back. He had watched afternoon cartoons for as long as I could remember.

Dr. Honey and my parents didn't understand. I noticed their expressions. They seemed to be saying, "Poor Christina, she really believes he'll wake up. She'll be hurt the worst when he dies. Poor Christina."

Where was their faith?

"Could I spend some time alone with Stevie?" I said quietly.

"Sure." Dr. Honey answered. "Just let us know when you're ready to go back to your room."

"I think I can manage this wheelchair alone," I told them.

As they turned to leave, I remembered that Mom and Dad had wanted to be with me in Steven's room. I imagined they had spent a lot of time there already. But, I had to be alone with him.

"Darling?" I whispered. "I'm here." I got as close to him as possible.

"I've been right down the hall. I just could never come to see you. Stevie, I'm really sorry."

"Why hadn't it been me?" I thought.

Tears came to my eyes. I tilted my head back in an effort to keep them from falling. I was determined to be strong for Stevie.

"Darling, I think you can hear me. Will you please wake up for me? Will you do that for me, Darling?"

He was still.

I picked up his hand and squeezed it tightly. "You know Stevie, I'm sure Grandma and Grandpa will let us spend the night at their house again. How would that be? I know how you love to look at the stars."

I went on talking to him for hours. Mom and Dad came in at one o'clock to tell me they were going to leave before the weather got any worse.

Dr. Honey came in at four o'clock to take me back to my room. I went with him only after a lot of urging and convincing.

Afterwards, when I was lying in my bed, the thought of Steven haunted me. I felt as if I needed more time with him. My visit had made me feel so helpless. I had believed that when I got a chance to be with him, he would suddenly wake up. I had no idea what to do for him now!

My faith did not falter.

Alone in my room, I said a prayer for Steven and hoped that my great-grandpa could also hear me.

"You said you would be here for me, and now, I really need your help," I said. "I've never stopped believing. You told me Stevie needed me, but I don't know what to do."

The distant thunder rumbled. Toward the hills I noticed trees bending with the force of the wind.

It was hard to ignore the pain from the surgery, but I had no time to think about that. I had to concentrate on Steven.

I finally fell asleep with an uneasy feeling nagging at my mind.

Chapter 15

With a sudden roar of thunder, I sat up in the dark. My ears were filled with the constant beat of rain bouncing off the window. An electric flash bathed the walls in a ghostly light.

I loved thunder storms. Especially when they happened in the summertime. The smell of electricity in the air, the warm rain, it was exciting! To me, God's display of his magnificent power was breathtaking.

Through my window, the glow of the city lights drowned out all but a few loney stars. But even they were overpowered by the lightning.

I listened to the thunder. It seemed to rise from the fiery depths of the earth and skake the surface in anger.

When my head finally lowered to the pillow, I

couldn't go back to sleep. I stared at the shadows around the room, kept awake by a feeling of distress. I couldn't quite pinpoint it.

Finally, it came to me. Steven was afraid of storms! The loud thunder had always scared him. He was alone in his room!

Quickly, I switched on the light with the controller. I had to get to Steven!

My room was bare. The wheelchair had been taken away. The crutches I was to use the next day hadn't arrived yet.

"I have to call nurse Henderson, "I thought, but hesitated. I knew that she wouldn't let me be with Steven that late. It was probably against the rules.

But Steven needed me!

In desperation I grabbed onto the metal safety bars on the side of the bed. I hung on for dear life as I swung my body over them. On the other side, my plan was to gently touch down on the floor with the support of my right leg. It didn't work.

I landed with a thud on the cold tile. My right leg had been too weak. Ignoring the pain, I pulled myself to the door. I quietly opened it. The nurses station was just down the hall. I could see Mrs. Henderson sitting at a desk.

"This is going to be some trick," I thought. It

took me a million years just to slide into the hallway and silently shut the door. I could see the eighth door at the end of the hall. Steven's room seemed so far away!

I started sliding backwards. Pushing off with my good leg and using my hands, I made it past the first three doors. Then I stopped to rest.

I caught my breath, deciding to still not acknowledge my pounding headache or the shooting pains in my left leg.

"I'm going to make it." I assured myself.

The next five doors passed ever-so-slowly, but with a lot of sweat, I made it.

Once in Stevie's room, I crawled up into a chair next to his bed.

Somehow, he didn't look as peaceful as he had earlier in the day. His hands were cold and damp, too.

"Stevie, don't be frightened," I whispered. "Darling's here." I held his hand.

When an earth-shaking boom of thunder shook the room, I thought I felt his hand tighten up. Maybe I imagined it.

"Darling, it's O.K." I thought about what I'd done to comfort him during the last storm. "Do you want me to sing you a song, Darling? How about your favorite? O.K.?"

Very softly, I began to sing.

"I looked out the window and what did I see?
Popcorn popping on the Apricot tree.
Spring has brought me such a nice surprise,
Popcorn popping right before my eyes.
I can take an armful and make a treat,
A popcorn ball that would smell so sweet.
It wasn't really so, but it seemed to be.
Popcorn popping on the Apricot tree."

The last note hung in the air. I had used the steady beats of the heart monitor to keep beat during the song. It continued without me.

After a while, I glanced at the clock. An hour had gone by.

"Grandpa?" I broke the silence. "Can you hear me? I've asked you over and over. Will you help me? If you will, please do it now. Steven deserves to live a long life. He is so innocent and caring. I know his love could touch so many people. But he has to live for that to happen. Please ---"

My heart jumped when a crackling silver light burst outside. I could see the sky turn from black to white each time the lightning blinked. When it ended, I listened.

Nothing!

The machines were quiet. The small night light had gone out.

"Steven!" I cried out in terror. "Oh, God, what's happened? Help us!"

My hands reached for the machine's panel. I wildly switched and pushed on buttons. Still nothing happened. The power had gone off.

"No, no, no!" I sobbed, out of control.

"Don't die! Don't die! Help! Someone!" I screamed. I pressed the 'nurse' button with a trembling hand.

Steven's little body lay motionless.

Tears poured onto my nightgown. Another blaze of lightning ripped the night. The room was lit up, revealing the white outline of my great-grandfather, standing over Steven. His hands had been placed on my brother's head and his eyes, closed.

"Had he come to take him away?" My mind raced with fear.

"No!" I screamed again, the thunder making my cries dissappear.

The machine had not come back on. I put weak arms on the edge of Steven's bed and a wet face on my arms. My whole body shook. With every breath, the word, "no" fell from my lips. I couldn't think, my clenched fists were my thoughts.

Footsteps and voices could be heard faintly out in the hallway, but I didn't listen to them, My heart dwelled in a different time and place. Every moment I had spent with Steven was replaying in my mind. I could hear him saying his first word and see him taking his first step.

The thunder grumbled long and low. As the sound faded, I thought I heard Steven's voice.

"Darling?" Again I heard him. "Don't cry, Darling. What's wrong?"

Slowly, I looked up. As I did, the machine began to function and the light popped and then glowed steadily.

Steven's eyes sparkled in the light as he stared back at me. I wiped my tears from my eyes and looked at him to make sure.

"I must be dreaming!" I thought.

"What's this?" Stevie asked innocently, touching the tube on his face. "What are we doing here?"

"Stevie! Darling, you're alive!" I wanted to leap up for joy, but I could only pull him close to me.

"Are you O.K.?" I asked.

"Yes, I'm fine. Why are you crying?"

"Oh Stevie, because I'm so happy!"

Chapter 16

Nurse Henderson rushed into the room and turned on the overhead light. What she saw made her mouth fly open. She hadn't expected to see me in the room, nor had she expected to see Stevie looking up at her. Quickly, she turned and hurried out.

"Who was that?" Stevie giggled.

"That was Mrs. Henderson. She's a nurse." I grabbed the phone on the night stand.

"Who are you calling?" Stevie wanted to know.

"I'm calling Mom and Dad." It felt like there were butterflies inside me! "Answer! Answer!" I coaxed. "Mom! It's me. Stevie woke up! ---I don't know. The power went out. The machines went off. I don't know how it happened! ---Bye!" I hung up when she said they'd be right over.

Nurse Henderson returned with a doctor and an orderly. She was out of breath.

"What do we have here?" the doctor asked.

Stevie smiled, taking everything in. Everyone returned his smile. This was a happy occasion. It was a miricle!

As for me, I was overjoyed! I said a silent "Thank you" prayer.

The doctor checked Steven's pulse and put a stethoscope to his chest. Nurse Henderson and the doctor carried on a cheerful conversation as they worked.

Suddenly, the nurse realized that I was out of place.

"Christina, how long have you been here? And how did you get down here?"

I laughed, "I managed. I had to be with Stevie. He needed me."

We were all too happy to worry much about how I got down there.

"How in the world did this happen?" Dr. Honey asked when he arrived.

"When I got here, this little guy was awake. Christina was with him. He seems fine. That's all I know." The doctor who had been there reported.

"Well, Christina," Dr. Honey said, rechecking

Steven. "What can you tell me? Why were you here anyway?"

Mom and Dad walked in. They both rushed over to Steven where he was sitting up on his bed.

"Oh, thank God!" Mom was crying.

Dr. Honey told them all he knew about what had happened.

"Chistina was just about to fill me in on the rest of the story."

They all looked at me, waiting.

"O.K., the reason why I am in here in the first place is because, ---well, I woke up and heard the storm. I was afraid that Stevie would be scared." I told them how I'd scooted down the hall and had been there when the power failed. I left out the part about Great-grandpa, deciding to tell Mom and Dad in private.

"What went wrong with the power?" Dad asked. "What happened to the generator?"

Dr. Honey explained that a circuit had been directly hit by the lightning and how, luckily, they were able to draw power from an emergency unit.

"It's no less than a miracle." Dad said.

Mom couldn't stop crying. I knew she realized what a mistake it would have been to end his life, and to think they almost did.

When Dr. Honey detached Stevie from all the life support paraphernalia, he could hardly believe Steven's remarkable recovery and restored health.

"This just does not happen," he said. "Christina, I've seen people who claimed to have faith. But in most cases, their friend or relative would have gotten well anyway. Then there's Steven. I hope that little fellow realizes what a wonderful sister he has in you. Your kind of faith is pretty special."

"Thank you, Dr. Honey. But special? Steven is the one who's special," I smiled.

My family celebrated by having a very early breakfast in the hospital cafeteria. While we ate, I told Steven that he had been asleep for a long time.

"We were in a little car accident on the way to Grandma's house," I explained. "You got a bump on your head. That's what made you fall asleep."

"Oh! Is that why you have that cast, Darling?"

"Yes. Today I get to use crutches so I can walk with the cast on." I answered.

"Will I use crutches, too?" Steven was serious.

"Well, no. You don't have a cast, but maybe Dr. Honey will let you try using some." I tried not to laugh at his question.

"Yay! Yay! Won-der-ful-to-me!" He laughed. "Wonderful-to-me" was his long-time expression of delight.

Dr. Honey came into the cafeteria and insisted that I go back to my room and get some sleep before I tried using crutches later on. I didn't like leaving Stevie, but Dr. Honey said that Stevie would be busy getting some tests anyway.

Dad pushed me to my room in a wheelchair.

"You get some rest," he ordered.

"Yes, sir!" I joked. Maybe now, finally, I *would* be able to rest.

Mom started to apologize. "Christy, I had no idea that this would happen. To think how close we came to letting him go. But you were right."

"Mom," I interrupted, "don't worry. I understand. You had no way of knowing."

I told them about Great-grandpa before they left. They accepted what I told them without question. After all that had happened, it was easy to accept the out-of-the-ordinary.

Once I was alone, I stared out the window. Pure, clear rays of the early morning sun spilled through the glass and onto the floor.

"Thank you, Grandpa," I whispered. "I knew you would help us." Then I remembered the unfinished business I had to take care of. "Could I ask one more favor? Would you please help a certain person be in a forgiving mood today?

Chapter 17

When Anna came in at eleven o'clock, I had fallen to sleep. She woke me up and congratulated me.

"I'm so happy for you!" She smiled broadly. "This is wonderful. I just heard the good news about Steven when I got to work. I know how much he means to you."

"Thanks, Anna. Do you know where he is right now?" I asked, groggily.

"He's going through a lot of testing, Dr. Honey's orders. Your mother is with him," she reported.

I was glad to hear that. "Will I be going home today?" I wasn't sure if the plans had changed.

"As far as I know." She picked up my chart from the end of the bed. "Yes, looks like you are still going home today, Christina."

"Not before I take care of one very important thing," I thought.

"Anna? Is Adam mad at me?" I questioned.

"No. He's hurt though. He doesn't know what he did wrong. I still can't understand, myself." She sounded a bit perturbed. After all, she didn't like seeing Adam hurt.

"I'm really sorry, Anna. I should have explained a long time ago." I said. Then after a moment, I tried to define my actions. "I felt guilty being with Adam. We had such a good time together. I thought that I was being unfair to Steven. I didn't want to be having a good time, when he couldn't. Do you understand what I mean?"

"I had a feeling it was something like that, but I'm not the person you should be telling this to," she said.

"Do you think Adam would talk to me?" I hoped that he would!

"Well, I'll see what I can do," Anna grinned.

"Thanks!"

Twelve o'clock arrived. Adam was on his lunch break. I watched the clock. Fifteen after, twenty after, ---

"Oh, what have I done?" I asked myself. "Adam was the sweetest person and I had just turned him away." I felt terrible.

At twelve-thirty the door opened slowly, but just a few inches. A white napkin, held by a hand, entered the room, waving.

"Peace?" the flag-waver said.

"Get in here, Adam," I laughed.

He walked all the way in. He came over to me and handed me a tiny purple flower.

"Here goes!" I thought.

"Adam," I began. "I ---"

"Wait! Anna told me," he smiled.

"She did?"

"I forced it out of her."

I could imagine him begging Anna and wished I could have seen him do it.

"Don't worry about it," he assured me.

"You mean you understand?" I couldn't believe it!

"Sure," he answered casually, "now that I know that that's what was bothering you."

What a relief that was!

"Thank you, Adam. This means a lot to me." I was having such great luck!

"I only ask one favor," he said. "I want to meet Steven."

"Sure. That's no problem." I really liked that

idea. I knew it would give me a chance to see Adam again.

We talked for the rest of his lunch break. We had a lot to catch up on.

The neatest thing happened just before he left.

"There's going to be a party at the Berrett Center on Saturday. Do you think you might want to go with me?" he asked, crossing his fingers.

"I'm going to be using crutches for the next ---"

"That's O.K. You'll be fine!" He assured me.

"I don't know." I wondered if I would be embarrassed using crutches in public.

"Oh, what the heck!" I thought.

"Sure." I smiled, bringing a relieved look to his face. "That would be fun."

"Great! I'll call you to give you all the details."

I was glad I had said yes.

"I'd better go," he announced. Suddenly, without warning, I got the biggest shock of my life, but not an unpleasant one. He bent down and gave me a kiss.

I couldn't say anything after that. I'm sure I was blushing.

"I'll talk to you later!" He hurried out as Anna came in with some crutches.

"Ooh," she teased, "you are both smiling. I guess that means things got straightened out between you two."

I ignored her little joke.

I quickly changed the subject. "You brought my crutches! Can I try them out?"

"Sure can!" she said.

Anna helped me off the bed. I took the crutches from her.

"All right, here I go." I took off around the room.

"Wow! You use those like a pro!" Anna laughed.

"I broke my leg when I was six. I've had some experience with these boards."

"Your parents and Steven are waiting downstairs."

"You mean we're leaving now?" I thought I had more time.

"Yes, are you ready?" She walked over to my nightstand where my "Marriage of Figaro" score lay. "Better not forget this!" She picked up my packed suitcase and opened it.

"We're going to miss you around here." She said, slipping the book into the suitcase and snapping it shut.

"I know, I'm going to miss you too, Anna. I don't think I'll be missing traction too much though." I would have laughed, but suddenly I didn't feel like laughing. It was a strange feeling. In a way I felt sorry I had to leave.

"Ready?" Anna broke the silence.

"I think so."

Just when I thought I would get to greet my family on crutches, an orderly showed up with a wheel chair.

"I don't need that," I told him.

"Sorry, Doctor's orders," he said. He sat me down and placed the crutches across the arm rests and headed toward the elevator.

When we arrived in the lobby, I was surprised to see Dr. Honey there with my family. In was harder than I thought saying good-bye would be. I had spent two weeks there. Dr. Honey and Anna had become like family.

"We'll be seeing you around here for a couple more months," Dr. Honey said to me. "You'll need therapy for that leg. And, before long we'll be removing those pins."

"Good-bye for now, then." I smiled.

Dad shook Dr. Honey's hand. "Thank you, for taking care of her." He turned to Anna. Thank you, too."

Dr. Honey bent down to Stevie and handed him a sucker.

"This is for being such a good patient through all of those tests."

"Thank you!" Stevie grinned.

After that, we said our good-byes once more and headed home.

Chapter 18

A few nights later, Stevie and I spent the night at Grandma and Grandpa's house. We had made up our minds once again to sleep in the back yard, under the stars.

As I lay there watching Steven gaze up at the sky, I thought about everything that had happened. I felt like I could face anything, after going through such a trial. I was so thankful Steven was with me, and was healthy.

I closed my eyes. Suddenly, I found myself looking at the apple tree! I could hear Grandpa's voice.

"Christina, I'm so proud of you! I knew you could do it! Look at all them apples! You've learned alot."

The tree had about twice as many apples as

before, and more roots were sticking out of the
ground.

"Well, good-bye Christina," I heard him once
again. "I'll see ya again."

I opened my eyes, happy and smiling. I *had* learned a lot. In a way, I even felt older, quite older.

The stars looked so pretty as they twinkled above
us. Somewhere, my great-grandpa was up there. I pictured him leaning against my apple tree.

"Darling?" Stevie said softly, could you tell me
again what the apples in the sky are called?"

"Stars, Darling."

"Oh, yeah. I'll have to remember that!"

But no one knew as well as I did, that there really
were apples in the sky. I had been lucky enough to
see mine.

"I love you, Darling," I whispered.

"I love you, too," came one sweet reply.

About The Author

Christina McDade was born in 1974 in Salem, Oregon and is growing up there. She attended Four Corners Elementary and Parrish Middle Schools. During these years, she was acting and singing in local children's theater groups.

She wrote her first novel, "Apples In The Sky", while a student of North Salem High.

"My family has always supported me no matter what I'm doing," she says. Just a few of her many "doings" include writing, voice and guitar lessons, maintaining "almost straight A" grades in accelerated classes, swimming , and attending 5:45 a.m. church classes before school.

Recently, Christina took Oregon State in an international 8th graders writing contest and was awarded $600.00 in a Fleet Reserve Contest for her Grand Prize essay, "What Patriotism Means To Me".

Christina's thoughts about her accomplishments: "I just feel so lucky that I've had the chance to do so much, even have my own book published, at age fourteen."

**********Author's note**********

Special Thanks

to my sister Sara, brother Shawn, my Darling Steven, Mr. Honey (my English teacher), and my friends: Laura, Matt, Gary, Joy, Heather, Danita, Jenny, and especially Teague, for letting me use your names in my first book.

How to order

If these items are not available in your local bookstore, you may purchase them by ordering directly from the publisher. Mail your order, with your check or money order to: Jordan Valley Heritage House, 43592 Hwy. 226, Stayton, Oregon 97383.

Children's books by Colene Copeland
(ages 6 thru 11)

Priscilla (hc) $8.95 plus $1.25 p&h per copy
Priscilla (pb) $3.95 plus $1.00 p&h per copy
Little Prissy and T.C. (hc) $8.95 plus $1.25 p&h per copy
Little Prissy and T.C. (pb) $3.95 plus $1.00 p&h per copy
Piston and the Porkers (hc) $8.95 plus $1.25 p&h per copy
Piston and the Porkers (pb) $3.95 plus $1.00 p&h per copy

Priscilla poster 15 x 20, Priscilla says,
"Pig Out On Books!" $2.50 plus $1.00 p&h per copy

Priscilla Presentation -- Video tape (VHS or Beta) This is the author at school, telling her side of the Priscilla story, what it was really like to raise a pig in the house.
Very funny! $29.95 postage paid
                                  rental -- $5.00 postage paid

Youth book by Christina M. McDade
(ages 10 thru 16)

Apples in the Sky (pb) $3.95 plus $1.00 p&h per copy

Thank you!   **postage credit issued